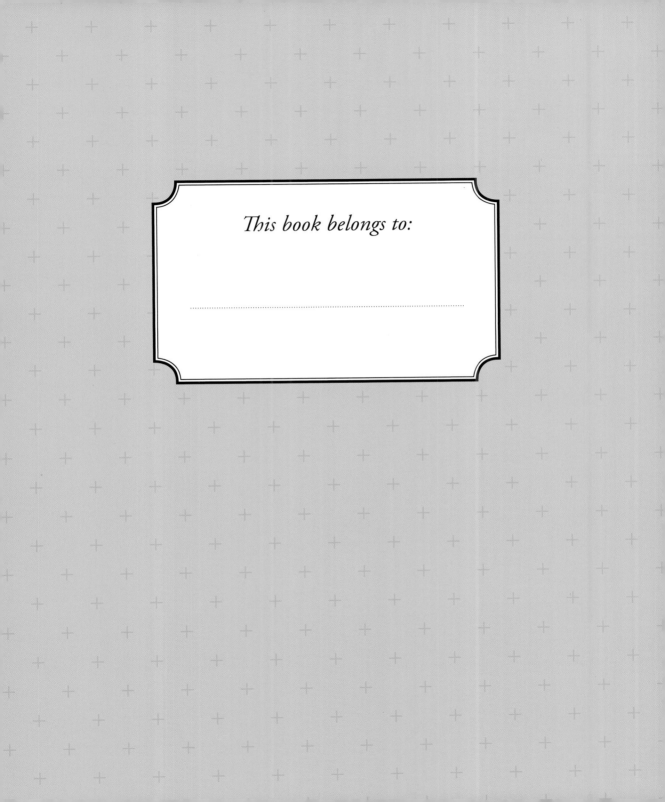

This book belongs to:

....

LADYBIRD
FAVOURITE
Nursery Rhymes

Illustrations by:
Mark Airs, Virginia Allyn, Jessica Barrah,
Sophie Fatus, Giuliana Gregori,
Desideria Guicciardini, Kirsteen Harris-Jones,
Siobhan Harrison, Ook Hallbjorn,
Agnieszka Jatkowska, Miriam Latimer,
Fernando Luiz, Maria Maddocks, Paul Nicholls,
Julia Patton, Marijan Ramljak, Andrew Rowland,
Angela Rozelaar, Emily Smith, Holly Surplice,
Natascia Ugliano, Kanako Usui,
Barbara Vagnozzi, Deborah van de Leijgraaf,
Richard Watson

Cover illustrated by Estelle Corke

LADYBIRD BOOKS

UK | USA | Canada | Ireland | Australia
India | New Zealand | South Africa

Ladybird Books is part of the Penguin Random House group of companies
whose addresses can be found at global.penguinrandomhouse.com.
www.penguin.co.uk
www.puffin.co.uk
www.ladybird.co.uk

Penguin
Random House
UK

First published 2012
This edition 2018
004

Copyright © Ladybird Books Ltd, 2012

Printed in China

A CIP catalogue record for this book is available from the British Library

ISBN: 978–0–241–37145–9

All correspondence to:
Ladybird Books
Penguin Random House Children's UK:
One Embassy Gardens, 8 Viaduct Gardens, London SW11 7BW

LADYBIRD
FAVOURITE
Nursery
Rhymes

Contents

ACTION
RHYMES

FOOD
RHYMES

COUNTING RHYMES

BEDTIME RHYMES

ANIMAL
RHYMES

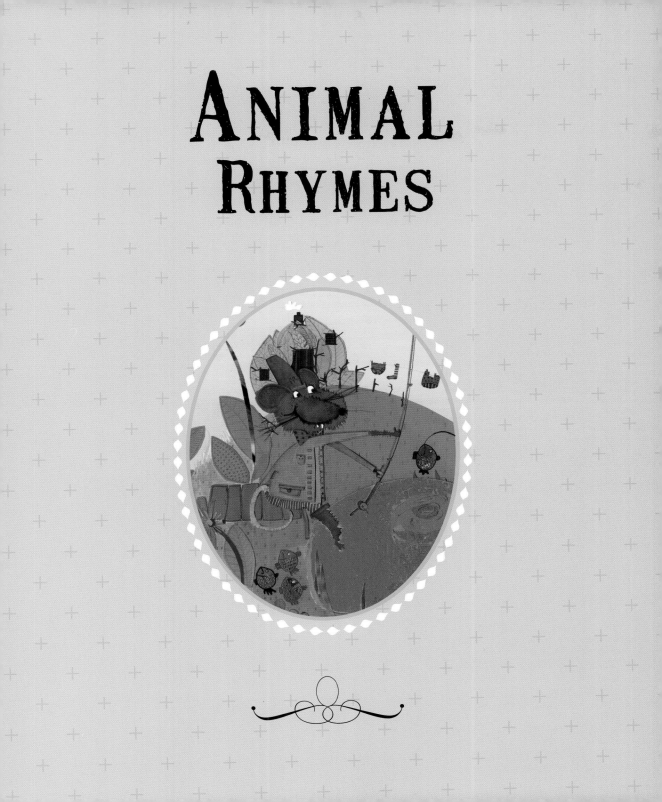

Mary Had a Little Lamb

Mary had a little lamb,
Its fleece was white as snow;
And everywhere that Mary went
The lamb was sure to go.

It followed her to school one day,
That was against the rule;
It made the children laugh and play
To see a lamb at school.

Baa, Baa, Black Sheep

Baa, baa, black sheep,
Have you any wool?
Yes sir, yes sir,
Three bags full;
One for the master,
And one for the dame,
And one for the little boy
Who lives down the lane.

Ride a Cock-Horse

Ride a cock-horse to Banbury Cross,
To see a fine lady upon a white horse;
With rings on her fingers,
And bells on her toes,
She shall have music wherever she goes.

19

Hickory, Dickory, Dock

Hickory, dickory, dock,
The mouse ran up the clock;
The clock struck one,
The mouse ran down,
Hickory, dickory, dock.

Ding, Dong, Bell

Ding, dong, bell,
Pussy's in the well;
Who put her in?
Little Johnny Green.
Who pulled her out?
Little Tommy Stout.

What a naughty boy was that,
To try to drown poor pussy cat,
Who never did him any harm,
And killed the mice in his father's barn.

Three Blind Mice

Three blind mice,
Three blind mice,
See how they run!
See how they run!
They all ran after the farmer's wife,
Who cut off their tails with a carving knife,
Did you ever see such a thing in your life,
As three blind mice?

Hey, Diddle, Diddle

Hey, diddle, diddle,
The cat and the fiddle,
The cow jumped over the moon.
The little dog laughed
To see such fun,
And the dish ran away with the spoon!

23

The Owl and the Pussy-cat

The Owl and the Pussy-cat went to sea
In a beautiful pea-green boat,
They took some honey, and plenty of money
Wrapped up in a five-pound note.

The Owl looked up to the stars above,
And sang to a small guitar,
"Oh lovely Pussy! O Pussy, my love,
What a beautiful Pussy you are,
You are,
You are!
What a beautiful Pussy you are!"

Pussy said to the Owl, "You elegant fowl!
How charmingly sweet you sing!
O let us be married! Too long we have tarried:
But what shall we do for a ring?"

They sailed away, for a year and a day,
To the land where the Bong-tree grows
And there in a wood, a Piggy-wig stood
With a ring at the end of his nose,
His nose,
His nose,
With a ring at the end of his nose.

"Dear Pig, are you willing to sell for one shilling
Your ring?" Said the Piggy, "I will."
So they took it away, and were married next day
By the Turkey who lives on the hill.

They dined on mince, and slices of quince,
Which they ate with a runcible spoon;
And hand in hand, on the edge of the sand,
They danced by the light of the moon,
The moon,
The moon,
They danced by the light of the moon.

Edward Lear, 1871

27

Little Bo-Peep

Little Bo-Peep has lost her sheep,
And doesn't know where to find them;
Leave them alone, and they'll come home,
Bringing their tails behind them.

28

29

Pussy-cat, Pussy-cat

Pussy-cat, Pussy-cat,
Where have you been?
"I've been to London
To visit the Queen."
Pussy-cat, Pussy-cat,
What did you there?
"I frightened a little
mouse under her chair."

Little Tommy Tittlemouse

Little Tommy Tittlemouse
Lived in a little house;
He caught fishes
In other men's ditches.

As I Was Going to St Ives

As I was going to St Ives,
I met a man with seven wives,
Each wife had seven sacks,
Each sack had seven cats,
Each cat had seven kits:
Kits, cats, sacks and wives,
How many were going to St Ives?

Cock a Doodle Do!

Cock a doodle do!
My dame has lost her shoe,
My master's lost his fiddlestick,
And knows not what to do.

Two Little Dicky Birds

Two little dicky birds,
Sitting on a wall;
One named Peter,
The other named Paul.
Fly away, Peter!
Fly away, Paul!
Come back, Peter!
Come back, Paul!

Bow, Wow, Wow

Bow, wow, wow,
Whose dog art thou?
Little Tom Tinker's dog,
Bow, wow, wow.

Hark, Hark, The Dogs do Bark

Hark, hark,
The dogs do bark,
The beggars are coming to town;
Some in rags,
And some in jags,
And one in a velvet gown.

Hickety, Pickety, My Black Hen

Hickety, pickety, my black hen,
She lays eggs for gentlemen;
Gentlemen come every day
To see what my black hen doth lay.
Sometimes nine and sometimes ten,
Hickety, pickety, my black hen.

Oh Where, Oh Where Has my Little Dog Gone?

Oh where, oh where has my little dog gone?
Oh where, oh where can he be?
With his ears cut short and his tail cut long,
Oh where, oh where is he?

The Lion and the Unicorn

The lion and the unicorn
Were fighting for the crown;
The lion beat the unicorn
All round about the town.
Some gave them white bread,
And some gave them brown;
Some gave them plum cake
And drummed them out of town.

A Frog He Would A-wooing Go

A frog he would a-wooing go,
"Heigh-ho!" says Rowley,
A frog he would a-wooing go,
Whether his mother would let him or no.
With a rowley, powley, gammon and spinach,
"Heigh ho!" says Anthony Rowley.

Goosey, Goosey, Gander

Goosey, goosey, gander,
Whither shall I wander?
Upstairs and downstairs
And in my lady's chamber.
There I met an old man
Who would not say his prayers.
I took him by the left leg
And threw him down the stairs.

The North Wind Doth Blow

The north wind doth blow,
And we shall have snow,
And what will poor Robin do then,
Poor thing?
He'll sit in a barn,
And keep himself warm,
And hide his head under his wing,
Poor thing.

Three Little Kittens

Three little kittens they lost their mittens,
And they began to cry,
"Oh mother dear, we sadly fear
That we have lost our mittens."
"What! Lost your mittens, you naughty kittens!
Then you shall have no pie."
"Miaow, miaow, miaow."
"No, you shall have no pie."

The three little kittens they found their mittens,
And they began to cry,
"Oh mother dear, see here, see here,
For we have found our mittens."

"Put on your mittens, you silly kittens,
And you shall have some pie."
"Purr-r, purr-r, purr-r,
Oh, let us have some pie."

The three little kittens put on their mittens,
And soon ate up the pie;
"Oh mother dear, we greatly fear
That we have soiled our mittens."
"What! Soiled your mittens, you naughty kittens!"
Then they began to sigh.
"Miaow, miaow, miaow."
Then they began to sigh.

The three little kittens they washed their mittens,
And hung them out to dry;
"Oh! Mother dear, do you not hear
That we have washed our mittens?"
"What! Washed your mittens, then you're good kittens,
But I smell a rat close by."
"Miaow, miaow, miaow.
We smell a rat close by."

Tom, Tom, the Piper's Son

Tom, Tom, the piper's son,
Stole a pig and away did run.
The pig was eat
And Tom was beat,
And Tom went howling down the street.

To Market, To Market, To Buy a Fat Pig

To market, to market, to buy a fat pig,
Home again, home again, jiggety jig;
To market, to market, to buy a fat hog,
Home again, home again, jiggety jog.

Ladybird, Ladybird

Ladybird, ladybird, fly away home,
Your house is on fire and your children all gone.
All but one, and her name is Ann,
And she crept under the frying pan.

Horsie, Horsie

Horsie, horsie, don't you stop,
Just let your feet go clippety-clop.
Your tail goes swish, and the wheels go round –
Giddy-up, we're homeward bound!

STORY
RHYMES

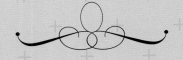

Rub-A-Dub-Dub

Rub-a-dub-dub,
Three men in a tub,
And how do you think they got there?
The butcher, the baker,
The candlestick-maker,
They all jumped out of a rotten potato;
'Twas enough to make a man stare.

Old King Cole

Old King Cole
Was a merry old soul,
And a merry old soul was he;
He called for his pipe,
And he called for his bowl,
And he called for his fiddlers three.

Georgie Porgie

Georgie Porgie, pudding and pie,
Kissed the girls
And made them cry;
When the boys came out to play
Georgie Porgie ran away.

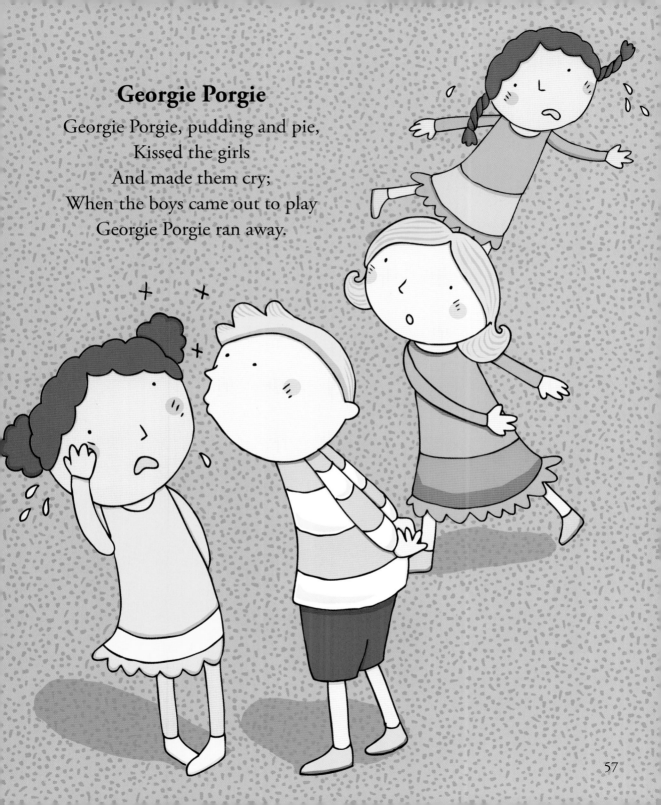

Polly, Put the Kettle On

Polly, put the kettle on,
Polly, put the kettle on,
Polly, put the kettle on,
    We'll all have tea.

Sukey, take it off again,
Sukey, take it off again,
Sukey, take it off again,
 They've all gone away.

59

There Was an Old Woman
Who Lived in a Shoe

There was an old woman who lived in a shoe,
She had so many children she didn't know what to do.
She gave them some broth without any bread,
Then scolded them soundly and sent them to bed.

See-saw, Margery Daw

See-saw, Margery Daw,
Johnny shall have a new master.
He shall have but a penny a day,
Because he can't work any faster.

Bobby Shafto

Bobby Shafto's gone to sea,
Silver buckles on his knee;
He'll come back and marry me,
Bonny Bobby Shafto!

Bobby Shafto's bright and fair,
Combing down his yellow hair;
He's my love for evermore,
Bonny Bobby Shafto!

Jack and Jill

Jack and Jill went up the hill,
To fetch a pail of water.
Jack fell down and broke his crown,
And Jill came tumbling after.

Frère Jacques

Frère Jacques, Frère Jacques,
Dormez-vous? Dormez-vous?
Sonnez les matines, sonnez les matines,
Ding dang dong, ding dang dong.

Humpty Dumpty

Humpty Dumpty sat on a wall,
Humpty Dumpty had a great fall.
All the king's horses
And all the king's men
Couldn't put Humpty together again.

67

There Was a Crooked Man

There was a crooked man
And he walked a crooked mile.
He found a crooked sixpence,
Against a crooked stile.
He bought a crooked cat,
Which caught a crooked mouse,
And they all lived together,
In a little crooked house.

The Grand Old Duke of York

Oh, the grand old Duke of York,
He had ten thousand men.
He marched them up to the top of the hill,
And he marched them down again.

And when they were up, they were up,
And when they were down, they were down,
And when they were only halfway up,
They were neither up nor down!

71

Lavender's Blue

Lavender's blue, dilly, dilly,
Lavender's green;
When I am King, dilly, dilly,
You shall be Queen.

72

Roses are Red

Roses are red,
Violets are blue,
Sugar is sweet
And so are you.

Little Miss Muffet

Little Miss Muffet,
Sat on a tuffet,
Eating her curds and whey.
There came a big spider,
Who sat down beside her,
And frightened Miss Muffet away.

74

Old Mother Hubbard

Old Mother Hubbard
Went to the cupboard
To fetch her poor dog a bone.
But when she got there
The cupboard was bare,
And so the poor dog had none.

75

Elsie Marley

Elsie Marley is grown so fine,
She won't get up to feed the swine,
But lies in bed till eight or nine.
Lazy Elsie Marley.

I Do Not Like Thee, Doctor Fell

I do not like thee, Doctor Fell,
The reason why I cannot tell;
But this I know, and know full well,
I do not like thee, Doctor Fell.

Doctor Foster

Doctor Foster went to Gloucester
In a shower of rain;
He stepped in a puddle,
Right up to his middle,
And never went there again.

Peter, Peter, Pumpkin Eater

Peter, Peter, pumpkin eater,
Had a wife and couldn't keep her;
He put her in a pumpkin shell
And there he kept her very well.

Peter, Peter, pumpkin eater,
Had another, and didn't love her;
Peter learned to read and spell,
And then he loved her very well.

Little Polly Flinders

Little Polly Flinders
Sat among the cinders,
Warming her pretty little toes;
Her mother came and caught her,
And whipped her little daughter
For spoiling her nice new clothes.

Peter Piper

Peter Piper picked a peck of pickled pepper;
A peck of pickled pepper Peter Piper picked;
If Peter Piper picked a peck of pickled pepper,
Where's the peck of pickled pepper Peter Piper picked?

Solomon Grundy

Solomon Grundy,
Born on a Monday,
Christened on Tuesday,
Married on Wednesday,
Took ill on Thursday,
Worse on Friday,
Died on Saturday,
Buried on Sunday,
This is the end
Of Solomon Grundy.

83

Tweedledum and Tweedledee

Tweedledum and Tweedledee
Agreed to have a battle,
For Tweedledum said Tweedledee
Had spoiled his nice new rattle.

Just then flew by a monstrous crow,
As big as a tar-barrel,
Which frightened both the heroes so,
They quite forgot their quarrel.

Tinker, Tailor

Tinker,
Tailor,
Soldier,
Sailor,
Rich man,
Poor man,
Beggarman,
Thief.

Tom, He Was a Piper's Son

Tom, he was a piper's son,
He learnt to play when he was young,
And all the tune that he could play
Was, 'Over the hills and far away';
Over the hills and a great way off,
The wind shall blow my top-knot off.

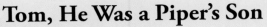

There Was an Old Woman Tossed up in a Basket

There was an old woman tossed up in a basket,
Seventeen times as high as the moon;
Where she was going I couldn't but ask it,
For in her hand she carried a broom.
"Old woman, old woman, old woman," quoth I,
"Where are you going to up so high?"
"To brush the cobwebs off the sky!"
"May I go with you?"
"Ay, by-and-by."

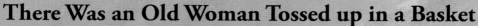

Sing a Song of Sixpence

Sing a song of sixpence
A pocket full of rye;
Four and twenty blackbirds,
Baked in a pie.

When the pie was opened,
The birds began to sing;
Wasn't that a dainty dish,
To set before the king?

The king was in his counting house
Counting out his money;
The queen was in the parlour,
Eating bread and honey.

The maid was in the garden,
Hanging out the clothes
When down came a blackbird
And pecked off her nose!

Curly Locks, Curly Locks

Curly locks, Curly locks,
Wilt thou be mine?
Thou shalt not wash dishes
Nor yet feed the swine,
But sit on a cushion
And sew a fine seam,
And feed upon strawberries,
Sugar and cream.

Hector Protector

Hector Protector was dressed all in green;
Hector Protector was sent to the Queen.
The Queen did not like him,
No more did the King;
So Hector Protector was sent back again.

Betty Botter Bought Some Butter

Betty Botter bought some butter,
But, she said, "The butter's bitter;
If I put it in my batter
It will make my batter bitter.
But, a bit of better butter
Will make my batter better."
So, she bought a bit of butter
Better than her bitter butter,
And she put it in her batter
And the batter was not bitter.
So, 'twas better Betty Botter
bought a bit of better butter.

Oh Dear, What Can the Matter Be?

Oh dear, what can the matter be?
Dear, dear, what can the matter be?
Oh dear, what can the matter be?
Johnny's so long at the fair.

He promised he'd buy me a fairing should please me,
And then for a kiss, oh! He vowed he would tease me,
He promised he'd bring me a bunch of blue ribbons
To tie up my bonny brown hair.

Oh dear, what can the matter be?
Dear, dear, what can the matter be?
Oh dear, what can the matter be?
Johnny's so long at the fair.

He promised to buy me a pair of sleeve buttons,
A pair of new garters that cost him but tuppence,
He promised he'd bring me a bunch of blue ribbons
To tie up my bonny brown hair.

Oh dear, what can the matter be?
Dear, dear, what can the matter be?
Oh dear, what can the matter be?
Johnny's so long at the fair.

He promised to bring me a basket of posies,
A garland of lilies, a garland of roses,
A little straw hat to set off the blue ribbons
That tie up my bonny brown hair.

There Was a Little Girl, and She Had a Little Curl

There was a little girl, and she had a little curl
Right in the middle of her forehead;
When she was good, she was very, very good,
But when she was bad, she was horrid.

Mary Had a Pretty Bird

Mary had a pretty bird,
Feathers bright and yellow,
Slender legs – upon my word
He was a pretty fellow!

The sweetest note he always sung,
Which much delighted Mary.
She often, where the cage was hung,
Sat hearing her canary.

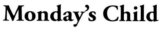

Monday's Child

Monday's child is fair of face,
Tuesday's child is full of grace,
Wednesday's child is full of woe,
Thursday's child has far to go,
Friday's child is loving and giving,
Saturday's child works hard for a living,
And the child that is born on the Sabbath day
Is bonny and blithe, and good and gay.

Bye, Baby Bunting

Bye, baby bunting,
Daddy's gone a-hunting
Gone to get a rabbit-skin
To wrap the baby bunting in.

101

What Are Little Boys Made Of?

What are little boys made of?
What are little boys made of?
Frogs and snails
And puppy-dogs' tails,
That's what little boys are made of.

What Are Little Girls Made Of?

What are little girls made of?
What are little girls made of?
Sugar and spice
And all that's nice,
That's what little girls are made of.

Little Boy Blue

Little Boy Blue,
Come blow your horn,
The sheep's in the meadow,
The cow's in the corn.
But where is the boy
Who looks after the sheep?
"He's under a haycock, fast asleep."
Will you wake him?
"No, not I,
For if I do,
He's sure to cry."

Jack Be Nimble, Jack Be Quick

Jack be nimble, Jack be quick.
Jack jump over the candlestick.

Simple Simon

Simple Simon met a pieman
Going to the fair;
Said Simple Simon to the pieman,
"Let me taste your ware."

Said the pieman to Simple Simon,
"Show me first your penny."
Said Simple Simon to the pieman,
"Indeed, I have not any."

Aiken Drum

There was a man lived in the moon,
Lived in the moon, lived in the moon
There was a man lived in the moon,
And his name was Aiken Drum.

And he played upon a ladle,
a ladle, a ladle
And he played upon a ladle,
and his name was Aiken Drum.

Cobbler, Cobbler, Mend my Shoe

Cobbler, cobbler, mend my shoe.
Get it done by half past two;
Half past two is much too late!
Get it done by half past eight.
Stitch it up, and stitch it down,
And I'll give you a half a crown.

Mary, Mary

Mary, Mary, quite contrary,
How does your garden grow?
With silver bells and cockle shells,
And pretty maids all in a row!

111

Miss Polly Had a Dolly

Miss Polly had a dolly
Who was sick, sick, sick,
So she called for the doctor
To be quick, quick, quick;
The doctor came
With his bag and his hat,
And he knocked at the door
With a rat-a-tat-tat.

He looked at the dolly
And he shook his head,
And he said "Miss Polly,
Put her straight to bed."
He wrote out a paper
For a pill, pill, pill,
"I'll be back in the morning
With the bill, bill, bill."

ACTION
RHYMES

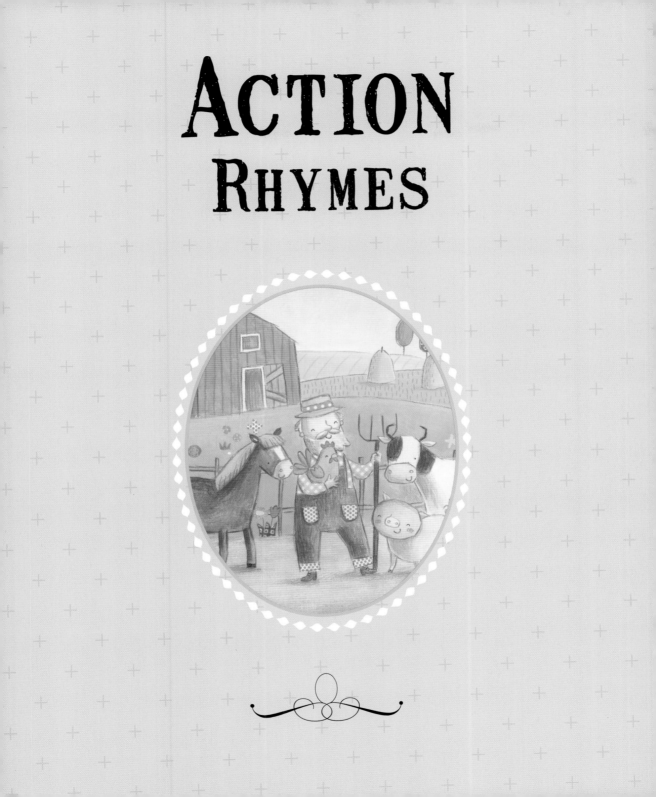

Teddy Bear, Teddy Bear

Teddy bear, teddy bear, turn around,

Teddy bear, teddy bear, touch the ground.

Teddy bear, teddy bear, climb the stairs,

Teddy bear, teddy bear, say your prayers.

Teddy bear, teddy bear, turn out the light,

Teddy bear, teddy bear, say goodnight.

117

Incy Wincy Spider

Incy Wincy Spider
Climbed up the water spout.
Down came the rain
And washed poor Incy out.

118

Out came the sunshine
And dried up all the rain,
And Incy Wincy Spider
Climbed up the spout again.

Head, Shoulders, Knees and Toes

Head, shoulders, knees and toes,
Knees and toes.
Head, shoulders, knees and toes,
Knees and toes.
And eyes and ears and mouth and nose.
Head, shoulders, knees and toes,
Knees and toes.

One Finger, One Thumb

One finger, one thumb
keep moving.
One finger, one thumb
keep moving.
We all stay merry and bright.

One finger, one thumb, one arm,
keep moving.
One finger, one thumb, one arm,
keep moving.
We all stay merry and bright.

One finger, one thumb, one arm, one leg,
keep moving.
One finger, one thumb, one arm, one leg,
keep moving.
We all stay merry and bright.

One finger, one thumb, one arm, one leg, stand up, sit down,
keep moving.
One finger, one thumb, one arm, one leg, stand up, sit down,
keep moving.
We all stay merry and bright.

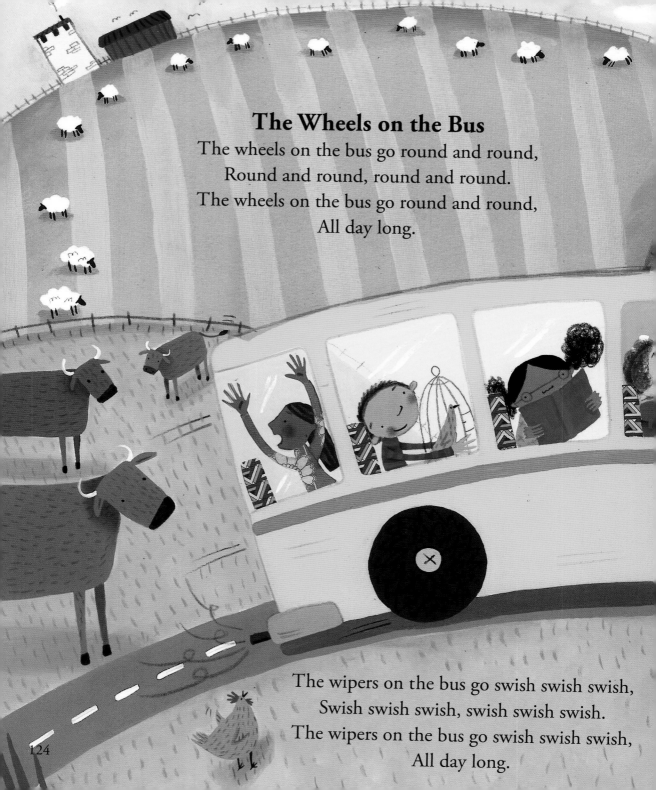

The Wheels on the Bus

The wheels on the bus go round and round,
Round and round, round and round.
The wheels on the bus go round and round,
All day long.

The wipers on the bus go swish swish swish,
Swish swish swish, swish swish swish.
The wipers on the bus go swish swish swish,
All day long.

The horn on the bus goes toot toot toot,
Toot toot toot, toot toot toot.
The horn on the bus goes toot toot toot,
All day long.

125

Ring-a-Ring o' Roses

Ring-a-ring o' roses,
A pocket full of posies,
A-tishoo! A-tishoo!
We all fall down.

Round and Round the Garden

Round and round the garden,
Like a teddy bear.
One step,
Two steps,
Tickle you under there!

127

One Potato, Two Potato

One potato, two potato,
Three potato, four,
Five potato, six potato,
Seven potato, more.

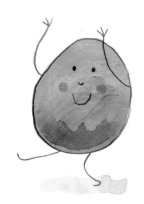

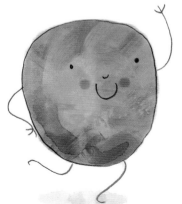

Here is the Church, and Here is the Steeple

Here is the church, and here is the steeple;
Open the door and here are the people.
Here is the parson going upstairs,
And here he is a-saying his prayers.

Oranges and Lemons

"Oranges and lemons,"
Say the bells of St Clement's.

"You owe me five farthings,"
Say the bells of St Martin's.

"When will you pay me?"
Say the bells of Old Bailey.

"When I grow rich,"
Say the bells of Shoreditch.

"Pray, when will that be?"
Say the bells of Stepney.

"I'm sure I don't know,"
Says the great bell at Bow.

Here comes a candle
To light you to bed.

Here comes a chopper
To chop off your head.

This is the Way the Ladies Ride

This is the way the ladies ride,
Nimble, nimble, nimble, nimble;
This is the way the gentlemen ride,
A gallop, a trot, a gallop, a trot;
This is the way the farmers ride,
Jiggety jog, jiggety jog;
And when they come to a hedge – they jump over!
And when they come to a slippery place – they scramble, scramble,
Tumble-down bump!

Row, Row, Row Your Boat

Row, row, row your boat,
Gently down the stream;
Merrily, merrily, merrily, merrily,
Life is but a dream.

Old MacDonald Had a Farm

Old MacDonald had a farm, E-I-E-I-O.
And on that farm he had a cow, E-I-E-I-O.
With a moo-moo here and a moo-moo there,
Here a moo, there a moo, everywhere a moo-moo,
Old MacDonald had a farm, E-I-E-I-O.

Old MacDonald had a farm, E-I-E-I-O.
And on that farm he had a pig, E-I-E-I-O.
With an oink-oink here and an oink-oink there,
Here an oink, there an oink, everywhere an oink-oink;
With a moo-moo here and a moo-moo there,
Here a moo, there a moo, everywhere a moo-moo,
Old MacDonald had a farm, E-I-E-I-O.

Old MacDonald had a farm, E-I-E-I-O.
And on that farm he had a horse, E-I-E-I-O.
With a neigh-neigh here and a neigh-neigh there,
Here a neigh, there a neigh, everywhere a neigh-neigh;
With an oink-oink here and an oink-oink there,
Here an oink, there an oink, everywhere an oink-oink;
With a moo-moo here and a moo-moo there,
Here a moo, there a moo, everywhere a moo-moo,
Old MacDonald had a farm, E-I-E-I-O.

135

Here we go Round the Mulberry Bush

Here we go round the mulberry bush,
The mulberry bush, the mulberry bush.
Here we go round the mulberry bush
On a cold and frosty morning.

This is the way we wash our hands,
Wash our hands, wash our hands.
This is the way we wash our hands
On a cold and frosty morning.

This is the way we wash our face,
Wash our face, wash our face.
This is the way we wash our face
On a cold and frosty morning.

This is the way we comb our hair,
Comb our hair, comb our hair.
This is the way we comb our hair
On a cold and frosty morning.

This is the way we tie our shoes,
Tie our shoes, tie our shoes.
This is the way we tie our shoes
On a cold and frosty morning.

This Little Piggy

This little piggy went to market,

This little piggy stayed at home.

This little piggy had roast beef,

This little piggy had none.

This little piggy cried, "Wee-wee-wee,"

All the way home.

FOOD
RHYMES

Little Jack Horner

Little Jack Horner sat in a corner,
Eating his Christmas pie.
He put in his thumb,
And pulled out a plum,
And said, "What a good boy am I!"

Pat-a-Cake, Pat-a-Cake

Pat-a-cake, pat-a-cake, baker's man,
Bake me a cake as fast as you can.
Pat it and prick it and mark it with B,
Put it in the oven for baby and me.

If All the World Were Paper

If all the world were paper
And all the sea were ink,
If all the trees were bread and cheese,
What should we have to drink?

Jack Sprat Could Eat No Fat

Jack Sprat could eat no fat,
His wife could eat no lean,
And so between them both, you see,
They licked the platter clean.

Dance to Your Daddy

Dance to your daddy,
My little babby,
Dance to your daddy, my little lamb;
You shall have a fishy
In a little dishy,
You shall have a fishy when the boat comes in.

147

The Queen of Hearts

The Queen of Hearts
She made some tarts,
All on a summer's day;
The Knave of Hearts
He stole the tarts,
And took them clean away.

The King of Hearts
Called for the tarts,
And beat the knave full sore;
The Knave of Hearts
Brought back the tarts,
And vowed he'd steal no more.

I Had a Little Nut Tree

I had a little nut tree,
Nothing would it bear
But a silver nutmeg,
And a golden pear;
The King of Spain's daughter
Came to visit me,
And all for the sake
Of my little nut tree.

151

Hot Cross Buns!

Hot cross buns!
Hot cross buns!
One a penny, two a penny,
Hot cross buns!

If you have no daughters,
Give them to your sons,
One a penny, two a penny,
Hot cross buns!

Pease Porridge Hot

Pease porridge hot,
Pease porridge cold,
Pease porridge in the pot,
Nine days old.
Some like it hot,
Some like it cold,
Some like it in the pot,
Nine days old.

Half a Pound of Tuppenny Rice

Half a pound of tuppenny rice,
Half a pound of treacle,
Mix it up and make it nice,
Pop goes the weasel!

154

Up and down the City Road,
In and out the Eagle,
That's the way the money goes,
Pop goes the weasel!

Oh, Have You Seen the Muffin Man?

Oh, have you seen the muffin man,
The muffin man, the muffin man?
Oh, have you seen the muffin man
Who lives in Drury Lane?

Oats and Beans and Barley Grow

Oats and beans and barley grow,
Oats and beans and barley grow,
Do you or I or anyone know
How oats and beans and barley grow?

Little Tommy Tucker

Little Tommy Tucker,
Sings for his supper:
What shall we give him?
White bread and butter.
How will he cut it
Without a knife?
How will he marry
Without a wife?

159

COUNTING
RHYMES

Five Little Ducks

Five little ducks went swimming one day,
Over the hills and far away.
Mother duck said, "Quack, quack, quack, quack,"
But only four little ducks came back.

Four little ducks went swimming one day,
Over the hills and far away.
Mother duck said, "Quack, quack, quack, quack,"
But only three little ducks came back.

Three little ducks went swimming one day,
Over the hills and far away.
Mother duck said, "Quack, quack, quack, quack,"
But only two little ducks came back.

Two little ducks went swimming one day,
Over the hills and far away.
Mother duck said, "Quack, quack, quack, quack,"
But only one little duck came back.

One little duck went swimming one day,
Over the hills and far away.
Mother duck said, "Quack, quack, quack, quack,"
And five little ducks came swimming back.

Five Little Pussy-cats Sitting in a Row

Five little pussy-cats sitting in a row,
Blue ribbons round each neck, fastened in a bow.
Hey, pussies! Ho, pussies! Are your faces clean?
Don't you know you're sitting there so as to be seen?

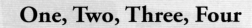

One, Two, Three, Four

One, two, three, four,
Mary at the cottage door,
Five, six, seven, eight,
Eating cherries off a plate.

Thirty Days Hath September

Thirty days hath September,
April, June and November,
All the rest have thirty-one,
Excepting February alone,
And that has twenty-eight days clear,
And twenty-nine in each leap year.

Five Currant Buns in a Baker's Shop

Five currant buns in a baker's shop
Round and fat with a cherry on top.
Along came a boy, with a penny one day,
Bought a currant bun and took it away.

Four currant buns in a baker's shop
Round and fat with a cherry on top.
Along came a girl, with a penny one day,
Bought a currant bun and took it away.

Three currant buns in a baker's shop
Round and fat with a cherry on top.
Along came a boy, with a penny one day,
Bought a currant bun and took it away.

Two currant buns in a baker's shop
Round and fat with a cherry on top.
Along came a girl, with a penny one day,
Bought a currant bun and took it away.

One currant bun in a baker's shop
Round and fat with a cherry on top.
Along came a boy, with a penny one day,
Bought a currant bun and took it away.

One, Two, Buckle My Shoe

1 **2**

One, two,

3 **4**

Three, four,

5 **6**

Five, six,

7 **8**

Seven, eight,

9 **10**

Nine, ten,

Buckle my shoe;

Knock at the door;

Pick up sticks;

Lay them straight;

A big fat hen!

This Old Man

This old man, he played one,
He played knick-knack on my thumb;
With a knick-knack paddywhack,
Give a dog a bone,
This old man came rolling home.

This old man, he played two,
He played knick-knack on my shoe …

This old man, he played three,
He played knick-knack on my knee …

This old man, he played four,
He played knick-knack on my door …

This old man, he played five,
He played knick-knack on my hive …

This old man, he played six,
He played knick-knack on my sticks …

This old man, he played seven,
He played knick-knack up in Heaven …

This old man, he played eight,
He played knick-knack on my gate …

This old man, he played nine,
He played knick-knack on my spine …

This old man, he played ten,
He played knick-knack once again;
With a knick-knack paddywhack,
Give a dog a bone,
This old man came rolling home.

There Were Ten in a Bed

There were ten in a bed
And the little one said
"Roll over, roll over!"
So they all rolled over
And one fell out.

There were nine in a bed …

There were eight in a bed …

There were seven in a bed …

There were six in a bed …

There were five in a bed …

There were four in a bed …

There were three in a bed …

There were two in a bed …

There was one in a bed
And the little one said
"Good night!"

Ten Green Bottles

Ten green bottles sitting on the wall,
Ten green bottles sitting on the wall,
And if one green bottle should accidentally fall,
There'll be nine green bottles sitting on the wall.

Nine green bottles …

Eight green bottles …

Seven green bottles …

Six green bottles …

Five green bottles …

Four green bottles …

Three green bottles …

Two green bottles …

One green bottle sitting on the wall,
One green bottle sitting on the wall,
And if one green bottle should accidentally fall,
There'll be no green bottles sitting on the wall.

One, Two, Three, Four, Five

One, two, three, four, five,
Once I caught a fish alive,
Six, seven, eight, nine, ten,
Then I let it go again.
Why did you let it go?
Because it bit my finger so.
Which finger did it bite?
This little finger on the right.

179

Five Little Peas in a Peapod Pressed

Five little peas in a peapod pressed;
One grew, two grew and so did all the rest.
They grew and they grew and did not stop.
Until one day the peapod popped!

Five Fat Sausages Sizzling in a Pan

Five fat sausages sizzling in a pan.
All of a sudden, one went bang.
Four fat sausages sizzling in a pan.
All of a sudden, one went bang.
Three fat sausages sizzling in a pan.
All of a sudden, one went bang.
Two fat sausages sizzling in a pan.
All of a sudden, one went bang.
One fat sausage sizzling in a pan.
All of a sudden, it went bang.
No fat sausages sizzling in a pan.

One For Sorrow

One for sorrow,
Two for joy
Three for a girl,
Four for a boy,
Five for silver,
Six for gold,
Seven for a secret never to be told.

One Man Went to Mow

One man went to mow,
Went to mow a meadow,
One man and his dog,
Went to mow a meadow.

Two men went to mow,
Went to mow a meadow,
Two men, one man and his dog,
Went to mow a meadow.

Three men went to mow.
Went to mow a meadow,
Three men, two men, one man and his dog,
Went to mow a meadow.

BEDTIME
RHYMES

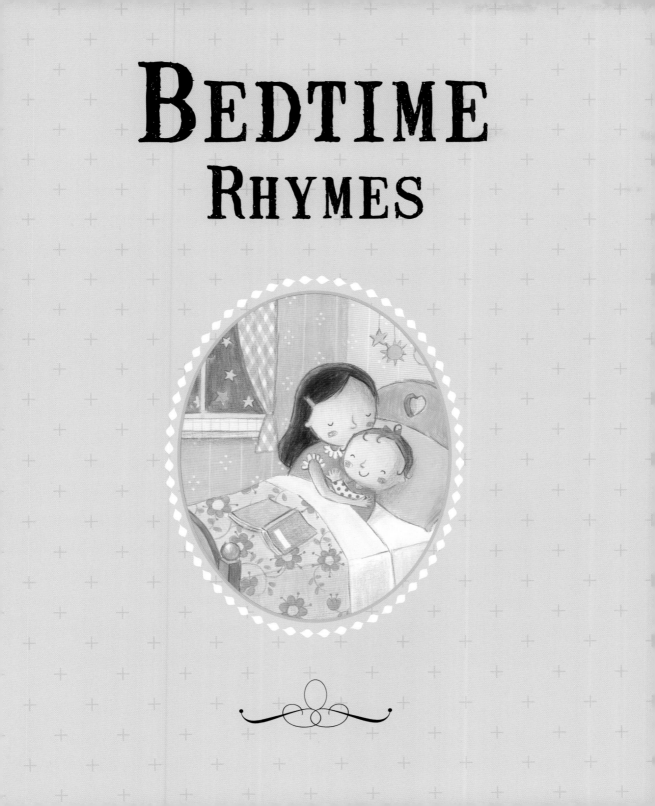

How Many Miles to Babylon?

"How many miles to Babylon?"
Three score miles and ten.
"Can I get there by candlelight?"
Yes, and back again.
If your heels are nimble and light,
You may get there by candlelight.

Twinkle, Twinkle, Little Star

Twinkle, twinkle, little star,
How I wonder what you are!
Up above the world so high,
Like a diamond in the sky.

When the blazing sun is gone,
When he nothing shines upon,
Then you show your little light,
Twinkle, twinkle, all the night.

In the dark blue sky you keep,
And often through my curtains peep,
For you never shut your eye,
Till the sun is in the sky.

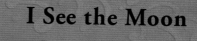

I See the Moon

I see the moon,
And the moon sees me.
God bless the moon,
And God bless me.

Star Light, Star Bright

Star light, star bright,
First star I see tonight.
I wish I may, I wish I might,
Have the wish
I wish tonight.

Sleepy-time Has Come for my Baby

Sleepy-time has come for my baby,
Baby now is going to sleep.
Kiss mummy goodnight,
And we'll turn out the light,
While I tuck you in bed
'Neath your covers tight.
Sleepy-time has come for my baby,
Baby now is going to sleep.

190

Sleep, Baby, Sleep

Sleep, baby, sleep,
Your daddy keeps the sheep.
Your mummy guards the lambs this night,
And keeps them safe till morning light.
Sleep, baby, sleep.

Sleep, baby, sleep,
Down where the woodbines creep.
Be always like the lamb so mild,
A kind and sweet and gentle child.
Sleep, baby, sleep.

Lullaby and Good Night

Lullaby and good night, mummy's delight,
Bright angels around my darling shall stand.
They will guard you from harms,
You shall wake in my arms.
They will guard you from harms,
You shall wake in my arms.

Golden Slumbers Kiss Your Eyes

Golden slumbers kiss your eyes,
Smiles awake you when you rise.
Sleep, pretty darlings, do not cry,
And I will sing a lullaby:
Rock them, rock them, lullaby.

Care is heavy, therefore sleep you;
You are care and care must keep you.
Sleep, pretty darlings, do not cry,
And I will sing a lullaby:
Rock them, rock them, lullaby.

Hush-a-Bye, Baby

Hush-a-bye, baby,
On the treetop,
When the wind blows,
The cradle will rock.

When the bough breaks,
The cradle will fall,
And down will come baby,
Cradle and all.

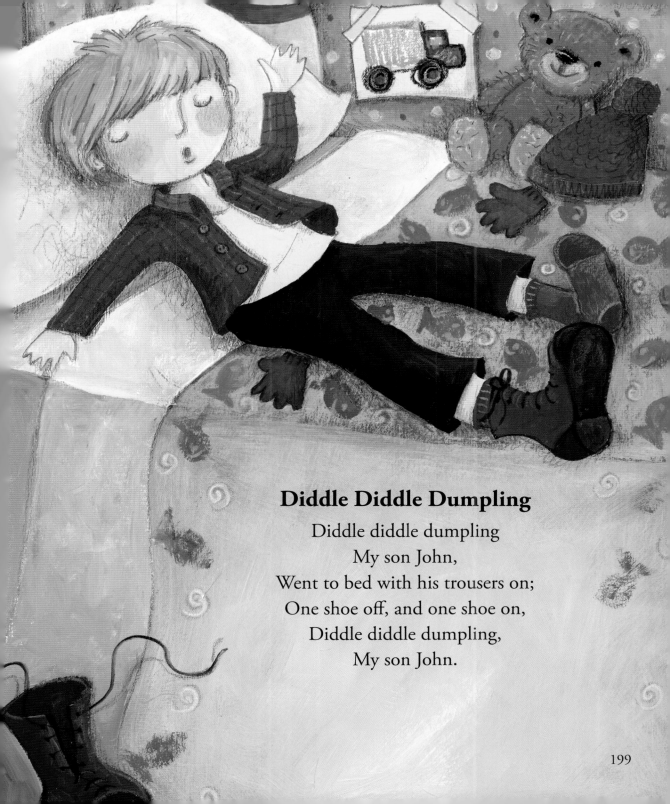

Diddle Diddle Dumpling

Diddle diddle dumpling
My son John,
Went to bed with his trousers on;
One shoe off, and one shoe on,
Diddle diddle dumpling,
My son John.

Girls and Boys Come Out to Play

Girls and boys come out to play,
The moon is shining bright as day.
Leave your supper and leave your sleep,
And come with your playfellows into the street.
Come with a whoop and come with a call,
Come with a good will or not at all.

Wee Willie Winkie

Wee Willie Winkie
Runs through the town,
Upstairs and downstairs
In his nightgown.
Rapping at the window,
Crying through the lock,
"Are the children all in bed?
For now it's eight o'clock!"

Rock-a-bye, Baby, Your Cradle is Green

Rock-a-bye, baby, your cradle is green,
Father's a nobleman, mother's a queen.
Betty's a lady and wears a gold ring,
And Johnny's a drummer, and drums for the king.

Niddledy, Noddledy

Niddledy, noddledy,
To and fro.
Tired and sleepy,
To bed we go.

Jump into bed,
Switch off the light,
Head on the pillow,
Shut your eyes tight.

207

How Many Miles to Babyland?

How many miles to Babyland?
Anyone can tell.
Up one flight,
To your right,
Please to ring the bell.

Up the Wooden Hill

Up the wooden hill
To Bedfordshire,
Down Sheet Lane
To Blanket Fair.

Come to the Window, My Baby, With Me

Come to the window, my baby, with me,
And look at the stars that shine on the sea.
There are two little stars that play at bo-peep,
With two little fishes far down in the deep,
And two little frogs cry, "Neap, neap, neap,
I see a dear baby that should be asleep!"

A Candle, a Candle

A candle, a candle
To light me to bed;
A pillow, a pillow
To tuck up my head.
The moon is as sleepy as sleepy can be,
The stars are all pointing their fingers at me,
And Missus Hop-Robin, way up in her nest,
Is rocking her tired little babies to rest.
So give me a blanket
To tuck up my toes,
And a little soft pillow
To snuggle my nose.

213

The Man in the Moon

The man in the moon
Looked out of the moon,
And this is what he said:
"Now that I'm getting up, it's time
All children went to bed."

214

Good Night, Sleep Tight

Good night, sleep tight,
Wake up bright in the morning light,
To do what's right with all your might.

215

In Winter I Get up at Night

In winter I get up at night,
And dress by yellow candle light.
In summer quite the other way,
I have to go to bed by day,
To go to bed by day,
To go to bed by day.

I have to go to bed and see
The birds still hopping on the tree,
Or hear the grown up people's feet
Still going past me in the street,
Past me in the street,
Past me in the street.

And does it not seem hard to you,
When all the sky is clear and blue,
And I should like so much to play,
To have to go to bed by day?
To go to bed by day?
To go to bed by day?

Index of first lines